ONE BEAR
IN
THE PICTURE

Caroline Bucknall

Dial Books for Young Readers · New York

To Sharon

First published in the United States 1988
by Dial Books for Young Readers
A Division of NAL Penguin Inc.
2 Park Avenue
New York, New York 10016
Published in Great Britain by Macmillan Publishers Ltd.
Copyright © 1987 by Caroline Bucknall
All rights reserved
Printed in Hong Kong
First edition
O B E
1 3 5 7 9 10 8 6 4 2

Library of Congress Cataloging-in-Publication Data
Bucknall, Caroline. One bear in the picture.
Summary: Though he wants to look
his best for the class photograph, Ted Bear
finds it very hard to stay clean.
1. Bears—Fiction. 2. Cleanliness—Fiction.
3. Schools—Fiction I. Title.
PZ7. B882337On 1988   [E]   87-6891
ISBN 0-8037-0463-1

Monday morning. Sleepy Ted
Was wishing he could stay in bed.

He brushed his teeth and combed his hair
And chose his favorite things to wear.

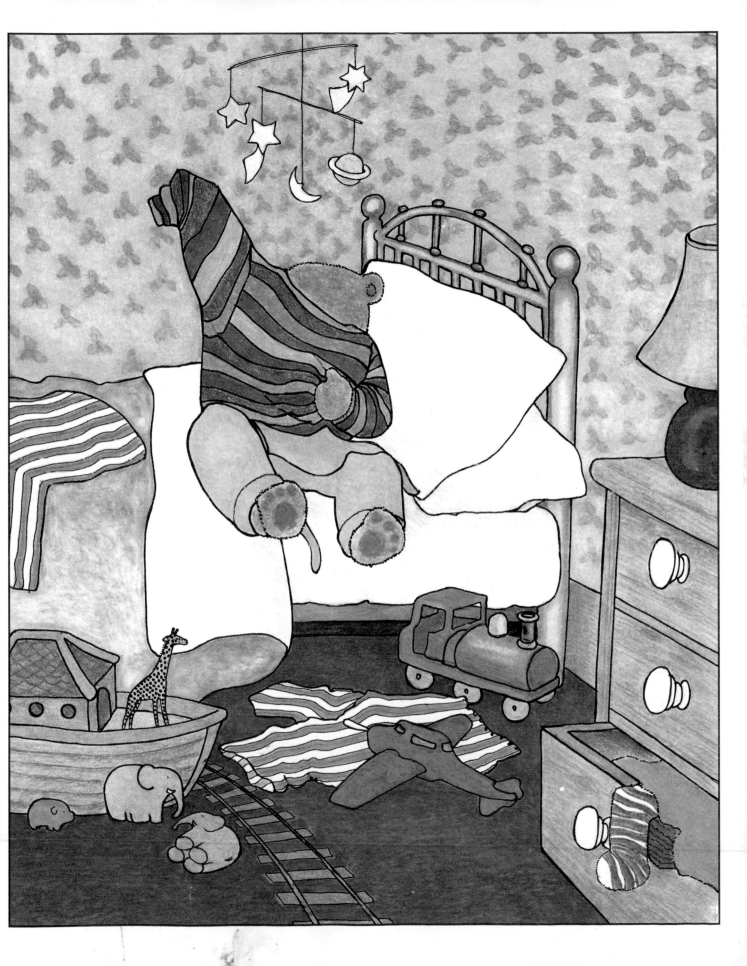

"I hope that you'll stay clean and dry,"
Said Mom at breakfast. Ted asked, "Why?"
"The school photographer is due
To take a photograph of you."

The careful bear did not forget.
It wasn't his fault he got wet.

Ted behaved himself in class,
But would the morning never pass?
"Will they take our pictures soon?"
The teacher said, "This afternoon."

At lunchtime Ted could not stay neat,
As bears are messy when they eat.

And staying clean when playing ball?
A bear cannot do that at all.

Purple, orange, black, and red—
Some on the painting, more on Ted.
While other bears in class were cleaner,
Ted was pink and blue and greener.

The magic moment came at last
To take a picture of the class.
The school photographer said, "Please…

Keep very still and all say 'Cheese'!"
The bears all had their pictures done,
First in a group, then one by one.

School was over. Time to go
Back home for cookies. Sadly, though,
It was the grubbiest of bears
Who crept past Mom and up the stairs.

I'd better give my clothes a scrub,
He thought, and climbed into the tub.
The soapy water washed away

The evidence of Teddy's day.
He dried himself a little later
Sitting on the radiator.

When Ted came down, he heard Mom say,
"How nice and clean you stayed today.
I just can't wait to see," she said,
"The picture of my spotless Ted."